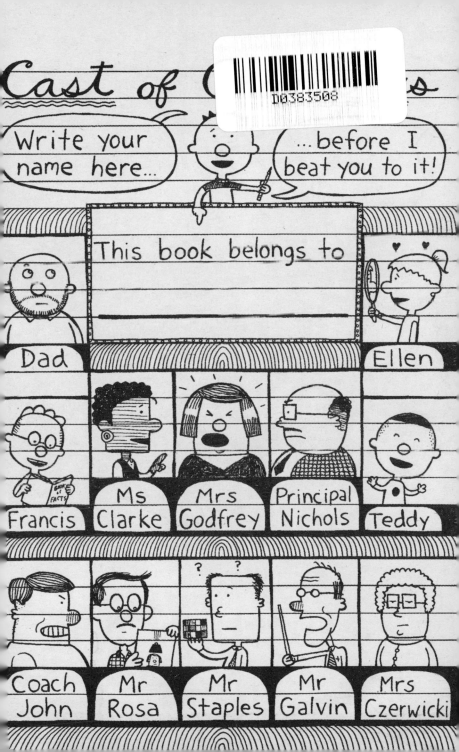

BiGNATE

THE BOY WITH THE
BIGGEST
HEAD
IN THE WORLD

First published in Great Britain by HarperCollins *Children's Books* 2010
HarperCollins *Children's Books* is a division of HarperCollins*Publishers* Ltd,
1 London Bridge Street, London SE1 9GF

The HarperCollins Children's Books website address is
www.harpercollins.co.uk

37

Text and illustrations copyright © 2010 by Lincoln Peirce

The author asserts the moral right to be identified as the author and
illustrator of this work.

ISBN: 978-0-00-735516-7

Printed and bound by
CPI Group (UK) Ltd, Croydon, CR0 4YY

Mixed Sources
Product group from well-managed
forests and other controlled sources
www.fsc.org Cert no. SW-COC-001806
© 1996 Forest Stewardship Council

FSC is a non-profit international organisation established to promote the
responsible management of the world's forests. Products carrying the FSC
label are independently certified to assure consumers that they come
from forests that are managed to meet the social, economic and
ecological needs of present and future generations.

Find out more about HarperCollins and the environment at
www.harpercollins.co.uk/green

For Jessica

Lincoln Peirce

is a cartoonist/writer and the creator of the comic strip *Big Nate*. It appears in more than two hundred U.S. newspapers and online daily at www.bignate.com.

Check out Big Nate Island at www.poptropica.com. And link to www.bignatebooks.com for more information about *Big Nate: In a Class by Himself* and the author, who lives with his wife and two children in Portland, Maine.

BiGNATE

THE BOY WITH THE
BIGGEST
HEAD
IN THE WORLD

HarperCollins *Children's Books*

CHAPTER 1

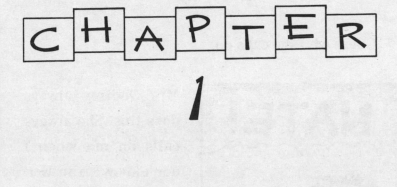

She could have called on anybody.

WHO CAN NAME THE SEVEN WONDERS OF THE ANCIENT WORLD?

There were twenty-two other kids in the classroom, and they all had their hands in the air. Francis did. Teddy did. Gina did, of course. Even Nick Blonsky, who usually sits in the back row with his pencil up his nose, had his hand raised. She could have called on one of them, right?

Guess who she calls on.

Mrs Godfrey always does this. She always calls on me when I don't know the answer. And she can TELL I don't know it. Ever hear somebody say that dogs can smell fear? That's Mrs Godfrey. She's like a dog.

A big, ugly, nasty dog.

I sort of skooch down in my seat. The whole class is staring at me. My ears start to burn, then my cheeks. I can feel tiny droplets of sweat beading up on my forehead.

o ° o° O ° °o O ° o ° O° O° o °O o ° O° o O ° O ° o O

"WELL?" she barks.

I've heard that on an average day, you use about ten per cent of your brainpower. Well, sitting here with my mouth turning as dry as a sack of sand, I really need that other ninety per cent to kick in. But my mind is blank.

Mrs Godfrey steps away from the whiteboard and starts towards me. She looks mad. No, worse than mad. She looks mean. Her face is flushed. I can see tiny flecks of spittle at the corners of her mouth. That's pretty gross. I brace myself…

And then the bell rings!

And rings. And keeps on ringing. Except it doesn't really sound like the school bell. It sounds more like…

I was DREAMING!! I blink hard, then let out a huge sigh of relief. I've never been so happy to hear that alarm clock in my entire life. Not that I'm ready to get up or anything. Closing my eyes again, I flop back down on to my pillow. ZZZZZZ...

Hey, thanks a lot, Dad. Way to break it to me gently. Nice parenting.

Actually, his parenting skills aren't that bad. He makes the nastiest tuna casserole you've ever tasted, but he's pretty harmless – especially compared to some of the psycho dads I've seen at Little League games. It's just that Dad's kind of clueless. He has no idea what it's like to be me.

I mean, how long has it been since he was in school – thirty or forty years? I think he's forgotten how it feels to be held prisoner all day long in a building that smells like a combination of chalk dust, ammonia, and mystery meat. He can't remember what it's like to be an average sixth grader.

PARENTAL FACT: *Once you go bald, you completely lose your ability to relate to anyone under the age of 30.*

Not that I'm an average sixth grader. OK, I'll admit that I'm not exactly Joe Honour Roll, but answer me this: When I get out there in the real world, is anybody

going to care whether or not I know who was vice president under Warren G. Harding? (And don't try to pretend that YOU know who it was, because you don't.) The point is, I want to use my talents for more than just memorising useless facts. I'm meant for bigger things. I am...

DESTINED FOR GREATNESS!

I'm still not 100 per cent sure what KIND of greatness I'm destined for, but I'll figure it out. I've got options. I keep a list on my closet door about this very subject.

There's also stuff I definitely WON'T achieve greatness in, like opera, synchronised swimming, and cat grooming. Enough said.

Let's get back to the unfortunate fact that today's a school day. But what KIND? You know, not all school days are created equal. You can rank them by category. (Just so you know, I'm really into ranking stuff. One time I spent a solid week ranking every kind of snack food I could think of. At the top: Cheez Doodles. At the bottom: rice cakes.)

DAD FACT:
Dad handed out rice cakes for Halloween one year. That was also the year our house got egged. Connect the dots, Dad.

HERE YOU GO, KIDS!

WHAT THE...?

If I were to grade the different kinds of school days report-card style, here's how they'd stack up:

A+ FIELD TRIP DAYS

I'm not talking about lame field trips, when a teacher makes you walk around the neighbourhood on Earth Day picking up litter. I'm talking about an all-day get-on-a-busand-go-somewhere field trip. Even if they give you a work sheet in the hope that you might actually learn something, you can usually come up with an excuse not to do it. That's what I did last year when we went to the aquarium.

B SPECIAL EVENTS DAYS

This is when classroom time gets eaten up by something better, like a movie or an assembly. Or, better yet, some sort of emergency. Last spring, Mrs Czerwicki's wig caught on fire and set

off the smoke alarm in the staff room. We got to evacuate the building and ended up playing ultimate Frisbee on the lawn for an hour. That was awesome. For everybody except Mrs Czerwicki.

C- SUBSTITUTE TEACHER DAYS

I think we can all agree that subs are almost always better than the real teachers. By "better" I mean "more clueless." The absolute best subs are the fresh-out-of-college ones who have never taught a day in their lives. Frankly, they're not very bright. Or maybe they're just really gullible.

D NORMAL DAYS

Unfortunately, most days are like this: You spend six-and-a-half action-packed hours studying subjects like photosynthesis and the War of 1812. Thrilling. You get home after school and your parents are like:

And you think about it for a solid ten seconds, and then you say:

F TRAIN WRECKS

There are so many ways for a school day to go wrong that it's almost impossible to list them

all. You could get screamed at by a teacher (usually Mrs Godfrey) for absolutely no reason, which seems to happen to me a lot. You could get roughed up by Chester, the school bully who looks like he spikes his chocolate milk with human growth hormone. Or your teacher could hit you with a quiz or a test you never saw coming...

Now there's a horrifying thought. Do we have a test today? I don't remember any teacher mentioning a test yesterday. But, like I already told you, I don't remember much of anything they say. I usually start to lose interest right around the time I hear:

SETTLE DOWN, CLASS.

("Settle down, class," in teacher speak, means "Let the mind-numbing boredom begin.")

It's times like this I wish I paid better attention in class. Like Francis.

Francis!!! HE'LL know whether or not we have a test today!

APPLE, CELERY, SANDWICH, YOGURT!

Here's the thing about Francis: He knows just about everything. He's always got his nose buried in the "Book of Facts," and he takes school pretty seriously. The truth is, he's kind of a geek. But I'm allowed to call him that because we're tight. We've known each other since the first day of kindergarten, when he started snoring during nap time. So I hit him in the head with my Thomas the Tank Engine lunch box, and we've been best friends ever since.

Let me see if he's up yet.

Yup, he's up. And he's reading, of course.

But… wait a minute! Look what he's reading!

So we MUST have a test today!!

This is bad. This is VERY bad. First, because my social studies textbook is in my locker at school.

And second, because I'm suddenly remembering what Mrs Godfrey said to me after our LAST test:

Yipe. We've got social studies first lesson. That only gives me about forty-five minutes to study my class notes.

AH! **HERE** THEY...

...ARE.

UH-OH...

18

Well, it looks like my class notes aren't going to be much help. Not unless Mrs Godfrey gives us extra credit for doodling.

I'm dead.

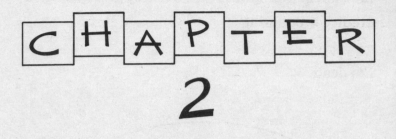

CHAPTER 2

"Breakfast is the most important meal of the day."

Have you ever noticed that's what people always say right before they stick a bowl of lumpy porridge in your face?

Now Dad's rambling on about how a high-fibre diet changed his life, but I'm barely listening. I'm still freaked out about this social studies test that could land me in summer school.

"Summer." "School."

Talk about two words that don't go together. Sort of like "porridge" and "breakfast."

Actually, I have no idea what summer school is even like. Francis thinks it's probably just like regular school, only hotter.

But other kids say that in summer school, the teachers make you work. And they're not talking about work sheets or chapter reviews. It's more like scraping gum off desks or scrubbing the toilets in the boys' changing room (which I hope isn't true, because those toilets are totally disgusting). It sounds pretty bad.

...AND AFTER THIS, MY CAR NEEDS WASHING!

The only kid I know who's ever gone to summer school is Chester. I guess I could ask him what it's like. Except the last time I tried to ask Chester something, he stuffed me into a rubbish bin. He's kind of a psycho.

KEEP OUR SCHOO CLEAN

ALL I ASKED WAS "CAN I BORROW A PENCIL?"

Whatever. The point is, summer school can't be good. I can't think of anything nastier.

Suddenly, right on cue… *IN WALKS ELLEN.*

OK, I CAN think of something – someONE – nastier. Summer school only lasts eight weeks. A fifteen-year-old sister is for ever. Until she turns sixteen, which is probably even worse.

Me and Ellen

Sisters don't have to be teenagers to be obnoxious, though. They're pretty much born that way.

If you have an older sister, you know exactly what I mean. You've been there. You feel my pain. If you DON'T have an older sister, congratulations. And welcome to my nightmare.

ELLEN FACT:
Every few months, she decides she doesn't like the way she laughs, so she changes it.

HA HA HA!... NO, THAT'S NOT RIGHT...

TOP 5 MOST ~ANNOYING~ THINGS ABOUT **ELLEN!**

5.) She is constantly begging Dad to buy her a cat.

We'll name her "Miss Kissy-kins"!

You want to know what else is annoying about Ellen? She doesn't have these types of problems. She's never had to worry about summer school because she's always been a good student. Which I get reminded of practically every day.

WHY CAN'T YOU BE MORE LIKE YOUR SISTER?

Right, like that's my goal in life: to be more like a high school cheerleader. Thanks, but no thanks.

Huh? Oh. Dad's talking again.

Note to self: Add "you can't shut her up" to list of annoying things about Ellen.

Hm. Don't think Dad really bought that. He's giving me "the Look."

THE LOOK
*Level One
on Dad's sus-
picion meter.
It means
he's not really
sure you're
being straight
with him.*

THE SQUINT
*Level Two
is basically
Dad's way of
saying, "You
can't possibly
be serious."*

**THE HAIRY
EYEBALL**
*Level Three
When Dad drops
a Hairy Eyeball
on you, look out.
Prepare for him
to go ballistic.*

Dad's only at Level One right now, but I can see where this is going. So I'd better get out of here before he asks any more questions.

ZOOM!

Whew! That was close. He has no idea I could end up in summer school.

Not unless he and Mrs Godfrey are having secret, late-night phone conversations.

Nice spot for a nap, Spitsy. Shouldn't you be off chasing squirrels or something?

Spitsy belongs to Mr Eustis, who lives next door. And, in case the doofy-looking dog sweater and giant funnel on his head didn't tip you off,

Spitsy is the ultimate dog nerd. He's afraid of postmen. He eats his own poop. And don't try throwing him a tennis ball. I did that once and we ended up at the vet

getting his stomach pumped. It's a long story.

But I don't want to pick on Spitsy. Spitsy's OK. After all, he's a dog, and all dogs are cool in my book. Except maybe those freaky little hairless Chihuahuas.

SPITSY FACT:
He has a crush on Francis's cat, Pickles.

It must be nice to be you, Spitsy. You get to hang out all day, sleeping in the sun. You don't have to worry about Hairy Eyeballs. Or big sisters. Or teachers.

...AND YOU ESPECIALLY DON'T HAVE TO WORRY ABOUT TAKING A SOCIAL STUDIES TEST.

SPITSY

WAIT a minute! Maybe *I* don't have to worry about the test either!

What if I can get out of it?

What if I can convince Mrs Godfrey to let me take the test tomorrow instead of today? Then I'll borrow Francis's class notes and cram for twenty-four hours. That'll at least give me a CHANCE to pass the stupid thing.

See, that's why dogs are so much better than cats. Cats never help you do ANYTHING. They just lie around the house, scratching up the furniture and licking themselves.

OK, brainstorm time. How can I get out of this test?

It's easy coming up with a plan. The problem is, almost as soon as I DO come up with a plan, I think of a reason it won't work.

PLAN A: ILLNESS

As soon as the test starts, I hold my breath until my face turns all red. Then I tell Mrs Godfrey I feel really, really sick.

WHY IT WON'T WORK

She keeps a thermometer in her desk.

JUST AS I THOUGHT: 37°!

PLAN B: INJURY

I wrap my hand in bandages, then tell her I can't write because I sprained my wrist.

WHY IT WON'T WORK

She'll make me take the test left-handed. Yup, she's that mean.

PLAN C: TRAGIC ACCIDENT

I pretend to hit my head against the door on my way into the classroom, then act like I've got amnesia.

WHY IT WON'T WORK

I used that one two weeks ago.

PLAN D: THE TRUTH

I walk right up to Mrs Godfrey, look her in the eye, and tell her that I didn't know there was a test today.

WHY IT WON'T WORK

The woman hates me.

Shoot. This is getting me nowhere. I've only got twenty-five minutes until the test. Twenty-five minutes until Mrs Godfrey brings down the summer school hammer on me.

I glance at my watch. Now it's twenty-FOUR minutes. Yikes.

It's beginning to look like the only way I'll be able to avoid this test is… is…

…is to skip school altogether!

CHAPTER 3

Yes! That's it! I'll skip school! I'll take the day off! I'll pretend somebody just invented a new holiday!

I'll stop right here.

What am I DOING? Nobody gets away with skipping school at P.S. 38. It's impossible.

Why? Two words: "THE MACHINE."

Not a REAL machine, like that funky-looking thing the caretaker uses to buff up the floors. The Machine isn't something you can see or touch. But it's there.

The Machine watches you. It knows your every move. And if you're not where you're supposed to be, the Machine tracks you down. Here's how:

1. THE SEATING CHART

Teachers always tell you where to sit. They claim it helps them remember kids' names. Right. Like they care what our names are.

They REALLY do it to keep tabs on you. One look at the chart and they know right away if you're not at your desk. Then the Machine starts up.

2. THE ATTENDANCE SHEET

Teachers write everything down. Who knows why.

They fill out an attendance sheet in every class. If you're missing, a big red "X" goes next to your name. Congratulations. You're absent.

3. THE CLASSROOM HELPER

We saw a movie about bees in science. This big fat queen bee sat around the hive doing nothing while the little drones did all the work. Sound familiar?

Teachers are the queen bees. Guess who the drones are.

It's always a suck-up like Gina who volunteers, because she's so desperate to earn extra credit. Good for you, Gina. I'm sure your career as a sixth-grade classroom helper will get you into some fancy-pants college.

TAKE THIS ATTENDANCE SHEET TO THE FRONT OFFICE.

The front office. The engine that runs the Machine. And right in the middle of it is...

4. THE SCHOOL SECRETARY

Mrs Shipulski's not so bad. It isn't HER fault they make her keep track of attendance. (I also don't blame her for all the times she says, "Nate, the principal will see you now.")

She's fast for an old lady. She looks over all those attendance sheets in no time. The second she spots that red "X" next to your name, she's on the phone to your parents.

There. You see how the Machine works? See how efficient it is? You can't win. There's no way to beat it.

That's my predicament. If I run off to the woods to hang out with Spitsy, it'll take about five minutes for Mrs Shipulski to fire up the Dad hotline. Then summer school would be the LEAST of my problems. I'd probably get suspended. Or expelled. Maybe shipped to some military academy where they slap a uniform on you, give you a buzz cut, and make you say "sir" at the end of every sentence.

BZZZZZ!

That settles it.

Skipping school is out. I need to be a little more creative about this. What I need is an excused absence.

An excused absence means you go to school just like normal, but you've got a parent note saying that you need to be somewhere else at a certain time. Bingo. You're free. Yesterday, Alan Olquist left halfway through science because he had to go and get a wart zapped. How lucky can you get?

So all I need to do is stroll into social studies with a note from Dad saying I've got an excuse – let's say a dentist appointment – and I'm off the hook. Genius!

Yeah, yeah. I know what you're thinking. I don't have a note from Dad. But I can take care of that.

> Dear Mrs Godfrey,
>
> Please excuse
> Nate from Social
> Studies at 8:45
> this morning.
> He has a very
> important dentist app

Whoa. Nope, that won't cut it. That looks too much like my handwriting. Mrs Godfrey will sniff that out right away. She may be loud and nasty, but the woman's not stupid.

I've got to make it look more like a grown-up's handwriting. Like DAD's. And his is wicked messy.

Whoops. Not THAT messy. Even *I* can't read that.

This is tougher than I thought it would be. And I'm running out of time.

Dear Mrs Godfrey,
    Please excuse Nate from Social Studies at 8:45 this morning. He has a very important dentist appointment.

Hey, HEY! THAT looks like the real thing! Pretty convincing!

Hello, excused absence! Goodbye, social studies test! All that's left to do is forge Dad's signature.

Uhhhh... Let me think about this for a sec. Forge. Forgery. Yikes.

Isn't forgery, like, a CRIME? Don't people get thrown in JAIL for signing the wrong name on a cheque or for using somebody else's credit card?

Listen, I'm no Goody Two-shoes. There's a desk in the detention room with my name on it – literally. But I'm not breaking the LAW. I don't want to get dragged out of P.S. 38 in handcuffs.

This might not be such a great idea. Maybe I should just rip this thing up before somebody comes along and…

Oh, man. It's only Francis.

That's the downside of living next door to your best friend. He's always sneaking up behind you and invading your privacy. Not that I have anything to hide.

OK, so I've got one tiny little thing to hide.

"Nothing?" he asks.

"Nothing," I shoot back.

"It doesn't LOOK like nothing."

Why is he acting all Sherlock Holmes on me?

I WAS FORGING AN EXCUSE NOTE...

...TO GET OUT OF TODAY'S SOCIAL STUDIES TEST.

Hmmm. Long, awkward pause. Francis has a weird expression on his face. One of those half-smiling, half-confused looks. He's either judging me for what I just told him, or he's about to fart.

"What social studies test?" he says.

Francis can be such a moron. (I've got to remind myself sometimes how smart he is.)

"The test I saw you STUDYING for this morning!"

"I wasn't studying for a test!" he says.

"Then why were you reading your social studies textbook?"

"Because I enjoy improving my mind!"

I'm going to ignore the incredibly lame statement Francis just made and focus on what he said right BEFORE that.

So… there's no social studies test?

THERE'S **DEFINITELY** NOT A TEST! I SH~~ ~~KNOW, BECAUSE I WRITE DOW~~ ~~YTHING SHE SAYS! IF WE ~~ ~~VE A TEST, I WOULD HAVE N~~ ~~IT WHEN I WAS REVIEWING MY N~~ ~~5 BLAH BLAH BLAH BLAH BLAH BLA~~ ~~LAH BLAH BLAH BLAB BLAB BL~~ ~~AB BLAB BLAB BLAH BLAH B~~ ~~LAH BLAH BLAH BLAB BLAB~~ ~~ BLAB BLAB…..

Yes!… YES!!…

"Actually," Francis says, his eyes getting all dreamy, "I sort of wish we WERE having a test today."

Sorry, Francis. But when you start acting like the mayor of Geek City, it's my job to knock some sense into you. You're lucky I didn't hit you with a heavier book.

There's the first bell. Not exactly music to my ears, but that sick feeling in the pit of my stomach is gone. No test! No summer school! This could end up being a half-decent day after all!

Yup, things are definitely looking up.

CHAPTER 4

"Hey, Nate! Taking a nap?"

OR ARE YOU DOING THE WORLD'S SLOWEST PRESS-UP?

That's Teddy. Just ignore his lame jokes. I always do.

Teddy's my OTHER best friend. Francis is #1, because I've known him longer. But Teddy is definitely #1A. He's awesome.

I wasn't so sure about him at first. That's the way it is with new kids. You sort of

TEDDY FACT:
He taught me how to say "Mrs Godfrey is fat" in Spanish.

¡ SEÑORA GODFREY ES GRASA!

¡ SÍ!

check them out from a distance to see if they seem cool or not. You don't want to be all Joe Friendly to them right away, because what if they turn out to be total losers?

Would you like to see my nasal spray collection?

Ok.

What am I SAYING?

random new kid →

← me

With Teddy, it was tough to tell. On his first day at P.S. 38, Principal Nichols asked me to show him around the school. Teddy was all quiet and serious. He barely said a word the whole day. I've told Teddy plenty of times since then that he seemed like a total dork.

Then he and I were paired up for a science lesson. We were supposed to dissect a squid.

We were about five minutes into it when Teddy picked up our squid and pretended it was a giant bogey.

It was hilarious. I started laughing…

…and then Teddy cracked up, too. That was the first time I'd ever heard him laugh. He sounded like some sort of crazed llama.

Oh, man. We lost it. We were laughing so hard that we dropped our squid on the floor. Then Mary Ellen Popowski stepped on it, which made us laugh even harder.

That's when Mr Galvin saw what was going on.
Wow, was he mad. He went Full Godfrey on us.

GLOSSARY
When a teacher com-pletely snaps and starts screaming, it's called a Full Godfrey. (When Mrs Godfrey does it, it's called Monday.)

He made us clean the squid guts off the floor. We apologised to Mary Ellen, but I guess we didn't sound sorry enough, because she kept whining that her shoes smelled like dead squid. I said maybe that was an improvement over how they smelled before.

Then I had to apologise to Mary Ellen AGAIN.

We had detention for two whole weeks.

You get in trouble that badly with somebody, and it changes the way you think about him. When I saw Teddy dangling that squid from his nose, I figured he was OK. And after we did all those detentions together, I knew we were going to be friends for life.

But that doesn't mean I'm going to let him beat me to the flagpole!

Ha! My turbospeed is taking over!

I'M GOING TO WIN THIS RACE BY A **MILE**!

Holy cow!! Principal Nichols!

This could get ugly. Principal Nichols is Mr Discipline. He doesn't stand for any horsing around. And here I am body slamming him on his way into the building. Stand back. He's about to explode.

Like I was saying: Principal Nichols – what a great guy!

"Are you all right?" he asks.

"Yeah. It didn't hurt," I tell him. "You're sort of like a giant air bag."

I'll just stop talking now.

"Move along, son," says Principal Nichols, looking like "son" is the last thing he wants to call me.

Whew. Sure, I'll be happy to move along. I thought he was going to hit me with a detention for sure.

"Come on, guys," says Francis. "Only a couple of minutes 'til homeroom."

I have sort of an organisation problem. One of these days I really need to clean out my locker. With a dumper truck. Or maybe a match.

But no time for that now. Let's see here… where's my lunch?

"I ran out of the house so fast this morning, I forgot to stick my lunch in my backpack!" I groan.

"No problem," Teddy tells me. "I've got you covered."

"You do?" I ask.

"Yup!" he says. "We went out for Chinese food last night. I've got a ton of leftovers."

Hm. A fortune cookie.

I like getting my fortune told. I'm well into horoscopes and Magic 8 Balls and stuff like that.

(By the way, I'm a Scorpio. That means I'm dynamic, loyal, and chock-full of animal magnetism. In other words, I rock.)

WHAT'S YOUR SIGN?

But fortune cookies bug me sometimes. Fortune-telling means predicting the future, right? But half the time, fortune cookies don't tell you ANYTHING about the future. They're just lame sayings.

Sometimes they're boring.

A large life is a series of small events.

CRUNCH CRUNCH

Sometimes they're stupid.

Hair today, gone tomorrow.

PLUS, THE COOKIES TASTE LIKE STYROFOAM.

Sometimes, like that time Dad took me and Ellen to Pu-Pu Panda, they make absolutely no sense. That one was so bizarre, I drew a comic about it:

I guess you could say I've got a love-hate relationship with fortune cookies. I hardly ever get a good one, but I still can't resist cracking 'em open.

Now THAT'S what I call a FORTUNE!

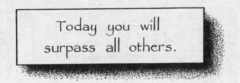

CHAPTER 5

I'm in an awesome mood when I walk into home-room. Not because of homeroom. Only a total geek would get all pumped about that.

See?

It's my FORTUNE that's great. It looked like today was going to stink out loud, and now everything's completely turned around!

"What are YOU so happy about?" Francis asks.

"I just got some amazing news," I tell him. "Have you ever heard me say I'm destined for greatness?"

"You may have mentioned it once or twice... or a zillion times," he says, rolling his eyes.

"Well, this PROVES it!" I say, handing him the fortune.

Francis reads it. He's making his constipated "I'm not so sure about this" face.

"Surpass all others?" he says. "Surpass them in WHAT?"

"I'm a man of many talents," I tell him. "It could be anything!"

Francis hands me back the fortune. "Not ANY-thing," he says with a smirk. "We can eliminate academic achievement as a possibility."

You're a riot, Francis. Just for that, I might not include you in my posse when I get rich and famous.

It'll be great to be rich. Then I can pay people to make my life easier. A chauffeur to drive me around. A brainiac to do all my homework. Somebody to buy all my clothes, so I don't have to go shopping and try on trousers in one of those cheesy little changing rooms. I hate that.

And I'll get a chef – somebody to cook me all kinds of good stuff. I'm STARVING right now. All I've got in my stomach is a couple of spoonfuls of lumpy porridge.

Hm. I guess I could eat this fortune cookie.

GINA!!!

Oh, how I hate her.

"Is this true, Nate?" Mrs Godfrey's voice cuts right through me as she heaves herself up from her chair.

Uh-oh. If Mrs Godfrey catches you eating in class, it's an automatic detention. Pretty bogus, considering she keeps a stash of peanut butter cups in her desk. (Don't ask me how I know that. I have my ways.)

Yikes. She's moving fast!
Come on! CHEW!

Swallow! NOW!!

Phew. Just in
time. I choke
down the last
few crumbs half
a second before
she steams up
to my desk.

"Hmmm," she says, looking long and hard. "I don't

see anything. You must have been mistaken, Gina."

HA!! Gina's speechless! Her little plan to land me in trouble didn't work! How sweet is THAT?

Oh, boy. Announcements. The excitement never stops around here.

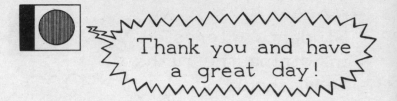

Thank you and have a great day!

That's it. Homeroom's over. So why am I still sitting here?

Because homeroom with Mrs Godfrey is followed by social studies with... MRS GODFREY! What a brutal way to start the day. Now I know where the phrase "rude awakening" comes from.

After social studies, there's nowhere to go but up. Here's the rest of my day:

LESSON 2: ENGLISH
Ms Clarke is OK, but shouldn't someone who teaches English actually make sense once in a while?

FOR A NONRESTRICTIVE CLAUSE OR PHRASE, BUT **NOT** FOR INDEPENDENT CLAUSES JOINED BY COORDINATING CONJUNCTIONS...

SAY WHAT?

LESSON 3: ART

This is my favourite class. Mr Rosa is so burned out, he doesn't even bother with lesson plans. Now that's teaching!

LESSON 4: LUNCH

You eat as quick as you can. Then you spend the rest of the time checking out girls and throwing carrot sticks at Brad Macklin.

LESSON 5: GYM

When you're playing hockey or dodgeball, it's awesome. When you're doing rhythmic gymnastics, you pray that nobody's around taking yearbook pictures.

LESSON 6: MATHS

Here's a multiple-choice question. Is maths:

A) totally boring?

B) completely useless?

C) a great place to grab an afternoon nap?

D) all of the above?

The correct answer, of course, is D. Which was also my grade on the last test.

LESSON 7: SCIENCE

The highlight of the year was when Mr Galvin's dentures fell out during his lecture on earthquakes. That's when I gave him the nickname "Shifting Plates."

I give ALL the teachers nicknames. I know: EVERYbody invents funny names for teachers. But I WORK at it. That's why I'm the official nickname tsar of P.S. 38.

A good nickname has a lot of stuff going on. One of my all-time best nicknames for Mrs Godfrey is Venus de Silo. (I got the idea from a famous sculpture called "Venus de Milo.")

Venus was the goddess of love and beauty. Mrs Godfrey isn't loving OR beautiful. So that makes it funny.

Venus is also the name of a planet. Mrs Godfrey is a lot like a planet. She's huge, round, and gassy.

A silo is filled with feed for cows. Mrs Godfrey reminds everyone of a cow, especially when she's eating.

And that's only ONE of her nicknames. I've got tons more. In fact, I can tell you exactly how many...

...AS SOON AS I CHECK MY LIST!

GODFREY NICKNAMES

1. Godzilla
2. Boring.com
3. Pass the Gravy
4. She Who Must Not Be Named
5. Dragon Breath
6. I Can't Believe She's Not Butter
7. Dark Side of the Moon
8. Extra Crispy
9. There's No Place Like Homework
10. Ozone
11. Queen Kong
12. Gas Station
13. Big Bang
14. Animal Planet
15. Wrecking Ball
16. Dullapalooza
17. El Guapo
18. Pardon My Nachos
19. Jaws
20. Venus de Silo

Twenty nicknames and counting! Not too shabby!

Yikes. Busted.

She looks at the list for a long time. Her face turns red, then white. I can see her jaw muscles working.

I wait for her to start shouting, but for the longest time she doesn't say a word. She just looks at me. That's worse than shouting.

Finally, she speaks.

She crumples up my list. Then she opens her desk drawer and pulls out a pad.

I've seen that pad before.

She writes something down, then hands me the slip. I notice a tiny smile at the corners of her mouth. But the rest of her looks mean.

"Take this to Mrs Czerwicki at the end of the day," she tells me.

DETENTION REPORT

STUDENT: _Nate Wright_

TEACHER: _C. Godfrey_

REASON FOR DETENTION:

Insolence

"Insolence?" I say out loud. "What's that?"

"Here's a dictionary," Mrs Godfrey snarls.

I bet it doesn't mean "destined for greatness."

CHAPTER 6

in·so·lence (ˈin(t)-s(ə-)lən(t)s), noun

1 : contemptuously rude or impertinent behavior or speech. **2 :** the quality or condition of being insolent.

"Turns out 'insolence' basically means acting like a brat," I say to Francis and Teddy as we walk to English.

I'm just about to give Teddy a notebook smack-down when I remember that he's going to share his lunch with me later. I decide to be nice to him.

SHUT UP, SCRUB.

I stuff Mrs Godfrey's detention slip deep into my pocket. I'm not going to let one little detention ruin my whole day. Especially not after I got such an awesome fortune.

"What do you guys think 'You will surpass all others' means?" I ask.

"Probably that you got somebody else's fortune cookie by mistake." Teddy laughs.

"It doesn't just say 'You will surpass all others,'" Francis corrects me. "It says, 'TODAY you will surpass all others'!"

Hm. He's right. So the fortune will probably come true during school. At home, the only "others" for me to surpass are...

…Dad and Ellen. Big whoop.

"So if the fortune is real," I say, "I'm going to sur-pass all others sometime in the next…"

"I guess so." Francis shrugs. "You'd better work fast."

Ugh. Jenny and Artur. Excuse me while I gag.

Thanks, Francis. Feel free to stop talking any time.

And, by the way, not EVERYBODY likes him. I'm not exactly president of the Artur Fan Club.

It's not like he's a major butthead or anything. I just hate that he's so GOOD at stuff – all the same stuff I'M good at. It's so obnoxious.

Things were a lot better before Artur came along.

ARTUR FACT:
He doesn't speak English all that great, which for some reason all the girls think is cute.

SEEING YOU LATERS!

SQUEAL!

HE'S ADORABLE!

Before Artur...	**After Artur...**
I was the #1 player on the chess team.	He knocked me down to #2.

Check-mate!

stunned expression

Nice tries, Nate!

Sigh...

So everybody thinks Artur is Mr Wonderful. I can deal with that. But when he and Jenny started going out? That killed me.

JENNY FACT:
She and Artur have been going out for four months, six days, and three-and-a-half hours. But who's counting?

I met Jenny in first grade. I've liked her ever since. And I'm positive that deep down she likes me, too, even though she ACTS like she hates me. I've always been 100 per cent sure that someday the two of us are going to make an awesome couple.

Then Artur comes along. The next thing you know, they're acting like Romeo and Juliet all over the place. It's gross. It's sickening.

The FORTUNE!

"Today you will surpass all others!"

Could that have something to do with Jenny? Maybe the fortune means I'm going to surpass Artur! Maybe Jenny dumps HIM...

"Today we'll be finishing up our poetry unit," Ms Clarke announces.

I used to think poetry was just a bunch of British dudes wearing tights and writing sonnets with a peacock feather, but there's a lot more to it. Ms Clarke has taught us about all kinds of poetry. We have to write our own poems in a "poetry portfolio."

POETRY! PORTFOLIO!
Nate Wright

LIMERICK by Nate Wright

I have feasted on all sorts of noodles,
I have tried an assortment of strudels.
Of the foods that I've eaten,
Only one can't be beaten:
An extra large bag of Cheez Doodles.

Nate
great ←
date ←
fate ←
late ←
mate ←
rate ←
state

HAIKU by Nate Wright

You have Cheez Doodles.
Fresh. Crunchy. Puffalicious.
Give me one right now.

Duh.

what rhymes with "Duh"?

ODE TO A CHEEZ DOODLE by Nate Wright

I search the grocery store in haste,
To find that sweet lip-smacking taste.
And there it is, in aisle nine.
It's just a dollar thirty-nine!
A bag of Doodles most delicious.
Check the label: They're nutritious!
And do you know how satisfied
I feel while munching Doodles fried?
I savour each bright orange curl,
Until it seems I just might hurl.
Their praises I will always sing.
Cheez Doodles are my everything.

Yee-HA!

QUACK

Doodle
oodle
noodle
strudel
poodle
caboodle

ON OFF

ZAP

Ms Clarke is still yakking away. "You may write any kind of poem you like," she says, "a funny poem, a serious poem, a love poem…"

JUNK food? Excuse me, but Cheez Doodles are NOT junk food. They're… YUMMY!

Hold it. Did Ms Clarke say "love poem"?

A love poem! That just might work! Jenny goes wild for that sort of thing. She was all excited about a valentine Artur gave her last year, and that was only a lame store-bought card.

I look across the room at Jenny. She's busy picking lint balls off her sweater, but there's electricity between us. I can feel it.

A plan is forming in my brain.

STEP 1: I write a love poem to Jenny – but not a sappy, mushy one. One that says, "Why hang out with Artur when I'M available?"

STEP 2: I slip the poem into Jenny's notebook, when Artur's not stuck to her like Joe Velcro.

STEP 3: I sit back and wait for Jenny to fall madly in love with me.

I've never written a love poem before. But how tough can it be? All I've got to do is find a few words that rhyme with "Jenny."

GINA!!!! Why can't she mind her own stinkin' business?

I can feel my face turning beetroot red. I sneak a quick peek at the other side of the room.

Jenny's looking at me funny. So is Artur. Great.

Leave it to Gina to ruin everything. Now my plan has exactly zero chance of working.

GOOD-BYE, LOVE POEM!

RIP!! RIP! RIP! RIP! RIP! RIP!!

NATE?

And now here's Ms Clarke. This just keeps getting better.

"Are you having trouble thinking of something to write about besides Cheez Doodles?" She smiles.

"Uh… yeah, sort of," I stammer.

"Poetry comes from the heart, Nate," she tells me. "That's where you'll find something to inspire you."

Uh, OK. I have no idea what she means, but I nod my head anyway. The whole class is staring at me.

I'm like, can we just move on?

Then I hear it. Nobody else does, but I do.

Gina laughs.

I shoot her a look. She's leaning back in her chair. She's got a nasty little smile on her face. Here I am looking like a fool in front of everyone – in front of JENNY – and Gina's loving every minute. SHE made this happen. This is her fault. The blood is pounding in my head. Ms Clarke is saying something. I can barely hear her.

What does my heart tell me?

It tells me…

CHAPTER 7

"So let me get this straight," Francis says as we file out of the English classroom.

GINA'S THE ONE WHO SHOULD KEEP HER BIG FAT MOUTH SHUT?

HEH HEH!

"Well, she SHOULD," I grumble, waving the pink slip Ms Clarke just handed me. "How come I get detention and GINA gets NOTHING?"

"Gina never gets in trouble," says Francis matter-of-factly. "She gets OTHER people in trouble."

Teddy takes the detention slip and reads out loud: "'Reason for detention: being disruptive in class, insulting a classmate.'"

Francis nods. "You WERE pretty insulting."

"Are you kidding?" I say. "That was NOTHING! I can be WAY more insulting than THAT!"

It's about to turn into a no-holds-barred yo mama throwdown when Francis interrupts us.

"Dudes!" he says, pointing excitedly. "Check it out!"

I look down the
hall. Check WHAT
out? Luke Bertrand
and Amy Wexler
are in a major lip-
lock…

Matt Grover is giving
Peter Hinkel a turbo-wedgie…

…and that weird girl
whose name I can
never remember is
writing all over her
arms again.

In other words, everything looks normal.

"What are we supposed to look at?" I ask Francis.

"Duh! The DISPLAY CASE!" he says.

P.S. 38 has two display cases. The one outside Principal Nichols's office is filled with all sorts of dusty trophies, boring spelling bee ribbons, and ancient pictures of the basketball team. (What's up with the UNIFORMS? It looks like they're wearing UNDERWEAR!)

P.S. 38 vs. DURHAM 1950

But the OTHER display case is cool. It's where Mr Rosa puts all the best student artwork. He always chooses one student to feature on the centre panel. There's a banner along the top that says:

If you've got the spotlight, it's like Mr Rosa's telling everyone...

Hey! That could be it!!

If something by ME is in the spotlight, that means the fortune was RIGHT! I'll surpass all others!

I rush up to the display case. I bet my penguin sculpture is there.

Yeah, LAME drawings. Time for some feedback from Nate Wright, Art Critic.

Nice try, Ken, but you should probably stick to woodwork.

Sorry to burst your bubble, Amanda, but this looks like a bunch of sausages with legs.

I'm not sure about THAT hand, Tammy, but your OTHER hand can't draw very well.

"AGAIN?" I blurt out. "This is the second month in a row he's been on the centre panel!"

"OLD SHOE" BY ARTUR

"Well, you have to admit," Teddy says, pressing up against the glass, "it's a pretty awesome drawing!"

"It's OK," I sniff.

"OK?" Francis protests. "He's like a junior Picasso!"

Oh, yeah? Since when did Picasso make a career out of drawing SHOES?

Yeah, yeah. Everybody loves Artur.

This is so unfair. Why should HE be such an art star? I've done TONS of drawings that are better than that stupid SHOE of his... Like THIS one!

"LUNCH"   by NATE

LOOK at that! My drawing has it all: Action. Suspense. Potential bloodshed. This deserves to be in the spotlight just as much as ARTUR's drawing! Time to file an official protest.

Wha—? Frivolous requests?? **FRIVOLOUS REQUESTS??**

Puppet heads? I'm supposed to concentrate on puppet heads NOW?? This is an OUTRAGE!

I glance up at the door. The display case is only a few feet away. If Mr Rosa won't put my drawing in that stinkin' case, I will.

Francis has his nose buried in the puppet head instructions:

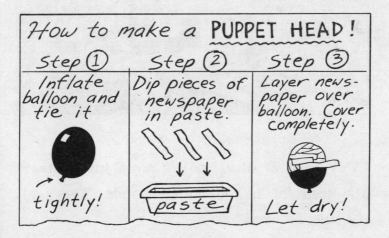

How to make a **PUPPET HEAD!**

Step ①
Inflate balloon and tie it
tightly!

Step ②
Dip pieces of newspaper in paste.
paste

Step ③
Layer newspaper over balloon. Cover completely.
Let dry!

He shoots me a suspicious glance. "Why are you whispering?"

"Ssh! No questions!" I hiss at him.

"ANY kind of diversion!" I say. "Just distract Mr Rosa for five or ten seconds. That's all the time I'll need."

"Need for… ?" he starts to ask, but I shush him. Mr Rosa is wandering over.

I give Francis a look that means: If you're REALLY my best friend, you'll do this for me.

He gives ME a look that means: You're a moron, but, hey, it's your funeral.

Good ol' Francis.

I ease over to the door. I wait for Francis to do his part.

PERFECT! The whole class cracks up, and while Mr Rosa is trying to calm everybody down...

I sneak out...

...and PRESTO! I'm standing in front of the display case! That was almost too easy!

Now I just have to pop open this door... and I'll stick MY drawing right on top of Artur's! HA!

You've gotta be KIDDING me! It's STUCK! I yank and yank, but nothing happens...

... UNTIL THE KNOB BREAKS OFF!!

Holy cow, that was loud! Hope nobody…

Guess what Mr Rosa pulls out of his back pocket?

Yup. A little pink pad.

I look at the slip he gives me. Where it says "Reason for Detention," he didn't even write anything.

He just drew a frowny face.

CHAPTER 8

It smells like egg salad, there aren't enough tables, and the walls are the colour of cat puke. But after the morning I just had, I've never been so happy to walk into the cafeteria.

CAFETORIUM

Sorry. "Cafetorium." What a stupid word.

"I can't believe Mr Rosa gave you a detention!" Teddy says. "That's the first one he's handed out all YEAR!"

"Chester took our table," Teddy says, and he's right. Chester's sitting where I always sit, looking like the picture of Java man in our science textbook.

"Well," I snicker, "let's just ask him nicely to move."

Right. We all know you don't ask Chester for favours. Not unless you want to lose a few teeth. The kid once beat up his anger management counsellor.

Finding somewhere else to sit could be sort of a challenge. Let's check out a few of our options:

We decide to sit with our good friend Todd.

Whoops. Sorry, dude. (Mental note: Chubby kid with red hair and freckles is Chad, not Todd.)

"What are you reading?" Francis asks.

"*The Complete Book of World Records*," Chad says.

My ears perk up. World records? Hmm!

"What do you mean, ANOTHER one?" Francis jokes.

I ignore him and pull the fortune out of my pocket.

"This doesn't say, 'You will surpass your class-mates at P.S. 38,'" I declare. "It says, 'You will surpass ALL OTHERS'!"

I start flipping through Chad's book. There's got to be some record I could break. I just need to find the right one.

"Longest fingernails?"
Nope.

"Most tattoos?"
Don't think so.

"Is there a record for goofiest hair?" asks Teddy.

"Shut up," I say.

"Speed eating?" says Francis, looking sceptical.

"LOOK! Here's a guy who ate sixty hot dogs in ten minutes! And THIS guy ate forty-five slices of pizza in ten minutes!"

Thank you, Captain Obvious.

So what can I use to set a speed-eating record? We're racking our brains when we notice some kids about to dump their trays.

I can't hear what Francis is saying, but a few seconds later he's back at our table with…

...GREEN BEANS!!

Green beans?

"We have PLENTY of green beans!" Francis says.

"Riiiiiight!" says Teddy, catching on… "Because nobody EVER eats their green beans!"

Suddenly Francis and Teddy are zooming all over the lunchroom, asking everybody:

Before I know it, a pile of green beans the size of Mt Everest is sitting on the table.

"Wait, these are NASTY," I say. "They look slimy."

"Perfect!" says Francis. "They'll slide right down!"

"I'm not hungry right now," I protest weakly. "Let's do this tomorrow."

This world record thing is beginning to seem a lot less cool. How did I get myself into this mess?

A crowd is beginning to gather. Francis sets his stopwatch. I guess there's no turning back now.

Ready…

Set…

I grab a fistful of beans and jam them into my mouth. Cold bean juice dribbles down my chin as I chew once, twice, then swallow. They taste disgusting, but they do kind of slide right down. I shovel in another mouthful.

...then another... and another.

ONE MINUTE DOWN!

NINE TO GO!

One minute??? I've only been eating for one minute?

Oohhhhhhhhhh... I don't feel so good.

The crowd is urging me on, but it's not working. My throat's all gaggy. I feel a little dizzy. Pieces of half-chewed beans are flying everywhere. Forget the world record; I'm hoping I don't throw up in front of half the school.

Uh-oh. I know that voice. Red alert.

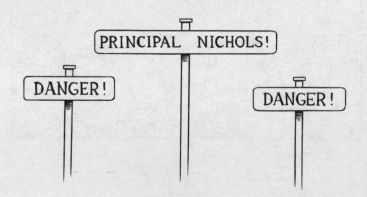

He was all nice and friendly when I ran into him earlier today. But he's not looking friendly now. My stomach does a triple somersault.

I start to talk, but this wad of beans in my mouth is cramping my style. I try to swallow it down, but I almost choke. It's just too big.

There's only one thing to do. I lean over the table and, trying to be as casual as I can...

...I spit out the beans.

OK, relax, people. It's not all THAT gross. A pile of chewed-up green beans looks about the same as a pile of UNchewed-up green beans.

Principal Nichols looks a little green himself.

"I'm just… er… having lunch," I say.

"Lunch?" he repeats. "With the entire sixth grade cheering you on??"

"Well, I'm declaring lunch officially over," Principal Nichols growls. He looks at the green beans scattered all over the table and floor.

He starts for the door, and in that half second I see exactly what's about to happen. It seems like it's in slow motion, but I can't do anything to stop it.

Principal Nichols's foot lands in a puddle of slimy bean juice,

AND...

For a minute, I can't tell if he's dead or alive.

Lucky me. He's alive.

And now I REALLY don't feel so good.

CHAPTER 9

Would it kill them to put a softer chair in here? This is like sitting on a toilet lid.

I try to ignore the pins and needles creeping down my legs. If Principal Nichols doesn't stop yakking soon, everything below my belly button will go numb.

He's lecturing me about the green beans. Yawn. I've heard this speech a zillion times. The words change a little bit, but it basically goes like this:

③ He uses the "P" word.

You have so much...
POTENTIAL!

And this is news?
Dude, I **KNOW** I have
potential. I'm just **SAVING**
it for something more
important than school.

TAKE THIS SLIP TO
MRS. CZERWICKI AT
THE END OF THE DAY.

REASON FOR
DETENTION:
GREEN BEAN
INCIDENT.

"Green bean incident"? That makes it sound like some sort of SCANDAL. Uh, HELLO? Earth to Nichols: I was trying to set a WORLD RECORD!

Not only that, his lecture dragged on past the fifth-lesson bell. Now I'm late for gym. Hey! Gym! THAT could be where I'll surpass all others!

Maybe I'm supposed to dominate in rope climbing or volleyball... or whatever Coach Calhoun has us doing today.

Except Coach Calhoun isn't here!

Coach John was P.S. 38's gym teacher back in the day. He retired, but the school keeps bringing him back as a sub. That might be fine for the school, but for us kids it's a complete nightmare. Because Coach John is insane.

COACH JOHN FACT:
He enjoys showing everyone the scars from all his knee surgeries.

...AND THE BONE WAS POKING THROUGH THE SKIN!!

RUN, MAGGOTS, RUN!

Have you ever seen one of those war movies where the drill sergeant is a total psycho who's always screaming at everybody? Take away the uniform, and you've got Coach John.

145

I sneak around the door, hoping to get into the changing room before he notices me. Not a chance. The man can't see his own feet, but somehow he spots ME right away.

Coach John's not really good with names.

See how warm and friendly he is?

I zip into the boys changing room. It's empty; that's a relief. Now I don't have to deal with Alan Ashworth and his Towel of Doom.

I jump into my shorts and T-shirt and head back to the gym when I spot myself in the mirror. I've still got dried green bean crud on my face. Nasty.

I'll just give it a quick rinse. I lean over the sink…

Oh, NO!!! There was water on the sink! It soaked right into my shorts!!!

I try to dry myself off with some paper towels, but it's no use. The spot's still there.

This is a DISASTER!! What am I gonna do?? I can't walk around like THIS! It's like carrying a huge sign that says:

I look around frantically for another pair of

shorts. Nothing in the lockers. Nothing in the lost and found. Suddenly I remember that JENNY'S in my gym class. She'll think I'm a total idiot!

"What are you doing, changing into a TUXEDO?" Coach John bellows. "GET OUT HERE!!"

...NOW!!

Gulp. Looks like I have no choice... **BUT WAIT!!!**

There's a duffel bag tucked under a bench near the coaches' room. And sticking out of it is...

A PAIR OF SHORTS!

YES! What LUCK! I peel off my wet shorts and grab the dry ones. I don't care whose they are, I don't care what colour they are, I don't care what size they are...

S M L

XXL XL

OK, maybe I DO care about the size thing.

Holy cow, these are like CLOWN clothes! They're not even CLOSE to fitting!

OK, KID! I'M GONNA COUNT TO TEN!

1...

2...

3...

Yikes. Coach John's getting ready to snap, big time. I've gotta find a way to make these shorts stay on, and fast.

4...

Aha! There's a pile of towels by the showers. I grab a handful...

5...

6...

C'MON!
C'MON!
FASTER!

GO!
HURRY!
GO!

7...

8...

9...

...and start stuffing them down the shorts!

152

I know I look like a Dorkosaurus. But I found a way to keep these shorts up. And they don't have a giant wet spot on them.

WADDLE
WADDLE
WADDLE
WADDLE

I hustle into the gym. The whole class is lined up in rows, stretching out.

HEH
HEH
HA
HA
HEE

I hear a chuckle. Then another one. In five seconds, everybody's laughing like crazy.

HA HA HA HA HA HA HA HA HA HA

Everybody but Coach John.

A joke? I have no idea what he means, but he looks like he's about to rip my arm off. I shake my head, afraid to say the wrong thing.

He slowly raises his hand and points at my shorts. I look at him, still baffled.

Then I see it.

A white "CJ" on Coach John's tracksuit.

I'm starting to get a very bad feeling. I look down at my shorts, and there it is: The same white "CJ."

Suddenly it hits me. Coach John thinks I'm making fun of him. That I'm showing off like I'm some sort of Coach John Mini-Me.

I can tell he's not hearing me. I can hardly hear mySELF. And all I can see is Coach John's giant face, turning about eight different shades of purple.

"We'll see if you're still laughing...," says Coach John,

...AFTER YOU'VE RUN SOME **GASSERS!**

Perfect. Just how I wanted to spend the lesson:

doing sprints.

In Coach John's shorts.

With a stomach full of green beans.

10

Another pink slip. This is getting ridiculous.

"Coach John gave me detention!" I say angrily.

"'No respect for teacher,'" I read aloud.

That's messed up. What about HIM having no respect for ME? He didn't even bother to write my NAME!

"What's so funny?"
I snap.

"He's right!" Francis
says. "You DO have weird hair!"

Great. Now, on top of everything else, my so-called best friends are treating my head like a giant Slinky.

This day is really starting to bum me out. "Any more of this," I grumble, "and today just might make my list of Worst Days Ever."

"Hold it," Francis points out. "You can't have a whole bunch of Worst Days Ever. By definition, there can only be ONE worst anything!"

Anyway, all I said was that today COULD make the list. It's not official yet. There's still a chance that this could turn into a GREAT day...

"I think you're trying too hard," Teddy declares.

"Whaddaya mean?" I ask.

"The whole FORTUNE thing! You're FORCING it! Just let it happen! ReLAX! Go with the flow!" Teddy says.

IN...
OUT...

IN...
OUT...

Go with the flow? What is this, a yoga retreat? I'm not going to surpass all others by sitting around doing deep breathing exercises.

"Let's move it, guys," says Francis. "We've got maths."

Ugh. I hate maths. I understand it fine, but my brain shuts down when Mr Staples says stuff like:

MATHS IS **ALL AROUND US!**

YOU'LL USE MATHS **EVERY DAY** FOR THE **REST OF YOUR LIFE!**

The rest of my life. I can't wait.

We head into the maths room. Right away, I can tell something's wrong.

Mr Staples isn't watering his plants or writing problems on the board. He's not chatting with students or telling them horrible knock-knock jokes.

Knock knock!

Who's there?

Woo.

Woo who?

Don't get so excited, it's just a joke!

"What's wrong with Mr Staples?" I whisper. "He's just SITTING there."

"Well, what's he SUPPOSED to be doing?" Teddy asks.

"Dancing on the desk?"

Teddy doesn't get it. But I do. I know trouble when I see it.

"Take your seats, everyone," Mr Staples says.

The classroom gets quiet. That's weird. Mr Staples NEVER tells us to take our seats. Suddenly everyone else is noticing what I've already realised: Something bad is about to happen.

"Please put away your books and binders," he instructs us.

"You have thirty minutes," Mr Staples says, passing out the quizzes. "Please read the instructions carefublah blah blah blah blah blah blah blah blah blah blah blah…"

While he babbles away, I quickly scan the quiz sheet.

Solve for the unknown value:
1. x ÷ 43 = 1,150
2. y ÷ 50 = 92
3. n ÷ 14 = 714
4. t ÷ 60 = 49

Find the mean, median, and mode:
5. 31, 169, 3, 38, 165, 105, 169, 64
6. 168, 44, 62, 25, 189, 26, 129, 92, 148, 62

Write each as a fraction:
7. 0.16
8. 0.36
9. 0.625

10. Twenty-one less than 4 times a number
     is 31. What is the number?

11. 2,000 and 11,000,000 added to a number is
     11,110,184. What is the number?

12. What is 5/9 of 6579?

Only twelve questions? Hey, that's not too bad!
I should be able to handle twelve questions in
thirty minutes.

...AAANND...

...BEGIN.

Mr Staples is done with whatever he was saying. He takes a look at the clock...

Away I go. Look, I already told you I'm not crazy about maths. But you don't have to LIKE something to be good at it. I work my way down the page.

This one's easy...

...and so's that one.

...and that one and THAT one. Holy cow, I'm CRUSHING these questions! This is a BREEZE!

I finish the last problem, check my answers, and put down my pencil. Done!

And check THIS out! I finished TEN MINUTES EARLY!

I look around the room.

Teddy's still working…

Francis is still working…

EVERYONE'S still working!!

I'm the first one finished! My superior brain-power has blown everybody else away. Hey! I'VE SURPASSED ALL OTHERS!

THE FORTUNE HAS COME TRUE!

OK, I'll admit that surpassing all others on a maths quiz isn't as exciting as setting a world record, but at this point I'll take anything.

I sneak a peek behind me. Even GINA'S still working! HA! I can't wait to see the look on her face when she realises that I ACED this quiz and SHE...

Yeah, hear that, everyone? Pass 'em in!

Wait. Check your answers front... and... back? Did he say BACK??

I flip my quiz over. My eyes feel like they're about to pop out of my skull.

There ARE! EIGHT more questions! Eight questions I DIDN'T EVEN SEE!!!

Everone else is handing in their quizzes. In a total panic, I grab my pencil. I don't even know what I'm writing. I just start scribbling numbers at random.

"I'll take that, Nate."

I flinch.

Mr Staples is standing at my desk. He grabs my paper.

NO!! I can't pass it in with almost half the questions BLANK! I pull the page away from him.

"Time's UP, Nate," he growls, trying to take it from me. I hang on tight. All I need is a couple more minutes!

But Mr Staples wants my quiz NOW. He pulls on the sheet hard. Suddenly I'm in a full-scale tug-of-war with my maths teacher.

And I just lost.

"I'll swap you," Mr Staples says through clenched teeth. He snatches the torn paper from my hand. "You give me THAT…"

A pink slip. All I was trying to do was finish the stinkin' maths quiz. Instead, here I am with another detention.

Teachers always say they'll be happy if you just do your best. But when you TRY to do your best, they don't LET you.

Something about that just doesn't add up.

CHAPTER 11

"This stupid fortune," I complain, crumpling the paper into a tiny ball, "has been nothing but trouble."

"How would your face like to entertain my fist?" I snap.

"Nate, the day's not over yet!" says Francis.

"Wake up, Rip Van Dorkle," I say. "Nothing good ever happens in science."

"Professor Chuckles," Teddy snickers. "That's funny."

"Don't let Mr Galvin hear you call him that," Francis says. "HE won't think it's funny."

"He never thinks ANYTHING'S funny!" I point out.

HE'S STIFF AS A BOARD.

"You can say that again," says Francis.

Something just CLICKED!

"Guys, that's IT!" I say excitedly. "The way for me to surpass all others! I'll do something NOBODY'S ever done! I'll make Mr Galvin LAUGH!"

Francis stares at me like he thinks I'm crazy.

"You're crazy," he says. "Don't you remember when we looked at all those old year-books in the library?"

Sure I do. We were trying to find funny pictures of teachers – bad haircuts, goofy-looking clothes, stuff like that. We dug out a bunch of yearbooks going back thirty or forty years. It was hilarious.

Mr Galvin's been teaching at P.S. 38 since the Jurassic period. (Another one of my nicknames for him is G-Rex.) So we found plenty of pictures of him.

There were formal shots. (Has Mr Galvin ever been INformal?)

There were candids. (You can't call them action shots since he's such a fossil.)

Mr Galvin – Science

"Stand back, everyone.
This bow tie is radioactive."

There was even a photo of him from his "hair replacement system" phase.

All the photos had one thing in common: Mr Galvin wasn't smiling in any of them.

"If nobody's ever seen him SMILE," Francis says as we head for the science lab, "how do you expect to make him LAUGH?"

"Hey, if anybody can do it, *I* can!" I say. "I crack people up ALL THE TIME!"

"Yeah, but not on purpose." Teddy chuckles.

RRRIIINNGGG!!

The bell. That's my cue.
Let the laughs begin!

I decide to start with
some good old-fashioned
visual humour. There's
nothing like a few strate-
gically placed pencils.

"Nuts," I say as I reach my desk. "No reaction."

"Here's a reaction," Teddy says. "I'll never, EVER borrow a pencil from you again."

"I'm just warming up," I say. "Watch THIS! I'm going to PLAN B!"

"Please open your textbooks to page…," Mr Galvin starts to say. I raise my hand.

"Mr Galvin? I have a science question for you," I say.

Wait, was that a hint of a smile? Did he start to laugh for just a half second?

Guess not.

"Psst! Mr Comedy!" Francis whispers. "You're BOMBING!"

"Butt out," I hiss back. "I still haven't hit him with my best material!"

I pull a page from my notebook. It's a "Doctor Cesspool" comic I've been working on, and it's almost done. I whip out my drawing pen and put the finishing touches on the last panel.

"Mr G.," I say, approaching his desk, "I have something to show you!"

He doesn't look up.

"Absolutely!" I answer. I hand him the comic. "The main character is a DOCTOR!"

He doesn't laugh. Pretty much the opposite, actually.

"You're wasting my time, young man," he says.

He jams my pen – my special drawing pen! – into his shirt pocket. Rats. I'll never see THAT again.

I trudge back to my seat.

"You're striking out, champ," Teddy whispers.

"You're just not tickling his funny bone."

It's worth a try. It's not like anything ELSE is working.

There's a feather duster over by the supplies cabinet. Mr Galvin uses it to keep the test tubes and beakers clean.

Easy now.
Gotta be casual
about this. I'll
just ease up
behind him

aaaannnnnnnnnnnnnnnnnd…

"I was… I was just… uh…," I start.

"QUIET!" he roars. "Just go to your desk and STAY there! And if I hear another PEEP out of you..."

...I'LL PUT YOU IN DETENTION FOR A WEEK!

What choice do I have? I shuffle to my desk, flop down into my chair, and stare straight ahead...

...at a tiny little dot on Mr Galvin's shirt.

The dot gets bigger... and bigger! ...and BIGGER!

My PEN!
The cap
must have come off inside his
pocket!

And here's the funny part: He
hasn't even NOTICED!

Yes, he has.

He stares me down. "Do you find this AMUSING, Nate?"

I know I should say no. Or at least try to keep a straight face. But something about that mondo ink stain on Mr Galvin's shirt is just... well...

I try to hold it in. I really do. But I can't. By the time I pull myself together, Mr Galvin is handing me a pink slip for five hours of detention.

Maybe someday I'll look back on this and laugh.

CHAPTER

12

It's 2:59.

School's over in exactly one minute. On a normal day, I'd be Mr Happy right about now. I'd be counting down the seconds, ready to jump out of my seat, making plans about how to spend the rest of the afternoon:

• Playing G-O-D-F-R-E-Y... (It's just like H-O-R-S-E, but it's **WAY** worse when you lose.)
CLANG!
ARGH!
HA! That's a "Y"!

• ...or dropping by Klassic Komix to buy the latest issue of *Femme Fatality*. ← best superheroine **EVER!!!**
You'll **LOVE** that one! It starts on the frozen planet of Gamma X-3...
DON'T RUIN IT!!

But there hasn't been anything normal about today since... since...

Hm. Guess the bell must have rung. Everybody's leaving.

As in leaving the building. Going home. And I'm not just talking about kids.

SO LONG, NATE! HAVE A NICE DAY!

"Have a nice day"? Is he serious? First of all, the day's over. Second, he already KNOWS I'm not having a nice day, since HE'S one of the people who STARTED this whole detention convention.

Teachers are such dopes sometimes. And by "sometimes," I mean "always."

The place empties out in no time. And before I know it...

...it's just me.

There's nothing more sickening than being stuck in school when classes are over. Try it sometime.

It feels totally wrong. You can almost hear the walls talking trash.

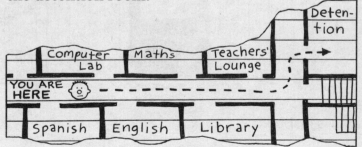

Shut up, walls.

No sense putting it off. I head for the detention room.

I admit I've had my share of detentions. I'm there so much, Teddy even made up a joke about it:

I didn't say it was a GOOD joke.

My last detention was the day of the chess club cake sale.

DRAMATIC FLASHBACK

Francis and I were running the table. We were making some pretty good money, mostly from selling Francis's mum's lemon squares, which are awesome.

NOTE: NOBODY WAS TOUCHING DAD'S COCONUT YOGURT PIE.

It was crowded. I noticed a kid named Randy Betancourt taking one of the lemon squares, real casual-like, and palming it in his hand.

He didn't pay. He just started walking away.

He acted all innocent. "Pay up for what?" he said.

He chucked the lemon square away, and…

…IT HIT MRS GODFREY!

Nobody had noticed me and Randy arguing, but EVERYBODY stopped and looked when that lemon square smacked into Mrs Godfrey's butt.

And of course she believed him. Shocker. Did she even ask for MY side of the story?

She pulled out her little pink pad and started writing. Randy stood beside her, giving me one of those "you got in trouble and I didn't" looks.

That's when I heard the voice inside my head:

GET YOUR MONEY'S WORTH

I was already getting detention, right? Might as well get punished for doing SOMETHING rather than for doing NOTHING.

So I did some-
thing.

DAD'S
COCONUT
YOGURT
PIE

I ended up with FIVE detentions that day. But I made sure Randy got what he deserved.

That's what bugs me about all the detentions I got today:

I walk in. Some days there are other kids, but today it's just me and Mrs Czerwicki.

MRS CZERWICKI FACT: *During detention, she passes the time by reading cheesy romance novels with titles like* Flames of Longing *and* Pounding Surf.

She puts down her book.

"AGAIN, Nate?" she asks with a sigh. I just shrug.

Did you hear that? "Slip." Singular. The old gal's pacemaker is about to get a major jolt.

"There's… uh… more than one, actually," I say, fishing in my pocket.

Mrs Czerwicki raises an eyebrow. "How MANY more?" she says.

I lay a wad of pink papers on her desk. It looks like a mutant origami.

"Nate," she asks, "just how many teachers gave you detention?"

"All of 'em," I say...

Mrs Czerwicki looks a little stunned. She spreads out the slips on her desk like she's playing solitaire.

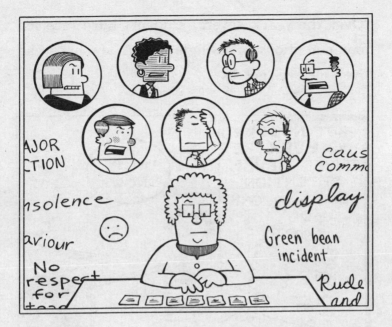

She shakes her head. "Nate…"

"Record?" I repeat. "What kind of record?"

"Over the years, several students have received four detentions in a single day. A few have had five. One even got six."

Wait. "Does that mean I've…"

Mrs Czerwicki grimaces. "Well… I suppose you could put it that way."

"It came true!" I shout.

"IT CAME TRUE!"

Mrs Czerwicki looks totally confused, which is nothing new. She takes off her glasses, rubs her eyes, and says, "Please sit down, Nate."

Sit down? Gladly! I practically dance over to my desk.

On the desktop, there's a drawing I made the last time I was here. (You're not supposed to draw on the desks, but what do they EXPECT us to do during detention? Just SIT here?)

Hey, I never SIGNED this! I sneak a glance to make sure Mrs Czerwicki's not looking. Then I pull out a pencil and write at the bottom:

by **Nate Wright**
SCHOOL <u>RECORD</u> HOLDER!

"School record holder."

NOW **THAT'S** GREATNESS!

OK, so it's not going to get me one of those display case trophies. But, hey, a record's a record. I'm officially a part of P.S. 38 history. When you think about it, getting all those detentions turned out to be pretty lucky.

I can hardly believe my good fortune.

BiGNATE
Comix by U! App

Create your own comix with art from BIG NATE! With your favourite characters, cool backgrounds, and fun props and sound effects, you can design your very own Nate-inspired comic strip.

The number of different comix you can make is infinite, so the possibilities are endless. As Nate says, your comix will "surpass all others"!

Includes five original app comix created by Lincoln Peirce himself!

Available on the Apple App store NOW - Search 'Big Nate Comix'.